This Is It

Catina Noble

crowecreations.ca

This Is It
© 2019 Catina Noble

First Crowe Creations Print Publication June 2019

Front cover photo by iStock
Cover Design © 2019 Crowe Creations
Interior design by Crowe Creations
Text set in Belfast SF; headings in Accent SF

Crowe Creations
ISBN: 978-1-927058-50-3

For the real Miss Tate.

Each friend represents a world in us, a world possibly not born until they arrive, and it is only by this meeting that a new world is born.—Anais Nin

This Is It

- 1 -

TEAL COULDN'T BELIEVE IT HAD been only a week since her father and Tonya's wedding and that things were finally getting back to normal. But now that all the hype was over, life seemed a tad on the dull side. The wedding had gone off without a hitch. Bonus. Toby had walked down the aisle with Teal and the crowd had gone wild over how adorable he was, all dressed up in his cute tuxedo. The wedding photos weren't as nerve racking as Teal had thought they would be, either. Another bonus. But there had been no honeymoon plans for the newlyweds. When Teal had inquired why, her father had told her it was because neither he nor Tonya had been able to get time off work, but the main thing was, they were still dealing with the final papers for Toby's adoption.

1

At least there was still Christmas to look forward to. Teal would have time with the family before worrying too much about applying for college and university. She'd spent the last couple of months pouring over catalogs, talking with her mother and father about her choices, and even with Jackson. Everyone had been supportive. In the end, though, it was Teal who had to decide what she wanted to do. Jackson had decided not to take a year off after he graduated from high school so was now attending Algonquin College. He was in his first year, in a general computers course, and had one more exam to do before he was officially finished his first semester. Teal was proud of him. She had to admit it made her feel quite mature to be dating someone who was in college when she herself was in high school, even if it was her last year.

Then there was the cost for college and university. The application fee alone was over a hundred dollars. And that fee was to apply to *either* college or university, not both. Nowadays, it seemed there was a fee for—in her mother's words—"every damned thing." Both her mother and father had some money put aside for her, and Teal was glad for that as she didn't think she could handle going to school full time and working a ton of hours on top of that. School had to be her top priority. She did not want to mess it up. There were so many things at stake. Maybe it was best that she put the whole college business out of her mind until after the Christmas holidays were over? Weren't the holidays stressful enough without adding anything to them? What about university? Should she try to get into that first, and then college could be her plan B? Like, if university didn't accept her, maybe she could go to college? What was the difference between the two? Heck, maybe she should consider taking a year off school. That idea sounded nice, but she knew that neither of her parents would ever let her do such a thing. She shook her head. She *had* to let this stuff go until the New Year.

"Okay, Toby. I'm ready!"

Three seconds later, Toby was running full speed into the kitchen, just as she'd expected. In fact, she would have been disappointed if he hadn't. He was, after all, officially her step-brother now that her father and his mother were married. Teal even had a small picture of "her little brother" that she carried around in her wallet. The picture had been taken at the park. She'd snapped it there when she babysat him once. In the picture, he sat in the sand, playing with cars and smiling up at the camera.

"Yay! Yummy." His eyes widened at the supplies he saw laid out before him: all the necessary ingredients for making a gingerbread house. Slabs of ginger, gummy bears, gumdrops, vanilla icing, chocolate icing, and gingerbread people. Teal had been looking forward to this. Now, she just needed to make sure Toby did not stuff most of the candy into his mouth while they made the actual house or else he'd be up all night running around in circles and she'd be the one who'd have to put him to bed. She was not feeling up to bedtime duty tonight.

She remembered one of the times she'd babysat. Toby had kept asking for more candy and squealed with delight each time she handed him a piece, so she continued giving him more. It was fun at first. One minute, he was clapping his hands and was happy and the next minute, he had puked all over the kitchen floor. The spew had gone everywhere. It had been so gross, Teal had nearly vomited when she attempted to clean up the mess. Of course, the whole time she was busy doing that, Toby was running around the house asking for more candy. Not only did she have to clean it all up, she had tried hard to keep the whole thing from her father's and Tonya's notice. She did not want them to think she'd been irresponsible. Lucky for her, Toby had just thrown up the once and they had spent the rest of the afternoon reading books and watching a movie, although just fifteen minutes into the movie he fell asleep on her lap. That was when she knew she loved the little sweetheart. At supper that night, he did not eat as much as usual, but enough that Tonya and Teal's father had not suspected anything and the whole babysit-candy-puke episode was still unknown to them. Teal hoped to keep it that way. Lesson learned. She would not let that happen again on her watch.

- 2 -

IT DEFINITELY FELT DIFFERENT HAVING a little kid around during the Christmas holidays. It made the whole holiday experience a lot more special and Teal enjoyed the season even more now that Toby and Tonya were around to share it with.

This year, it had been decided Toby would play the role of "Santa" and give out the presents to each person. That was fine with Teal. It was not like she was a kid anymore. She could wait to open her presents. All she had really hinted at, present-wise, was for a stereo and a gift card to the stationery store that Tonya had taken her to before. That way, she could pick out her own journals. Since Teal's wish list was never very long, more often than not, she got what she wanted for Christmas.

Teal saw Tonya give her father's leg a squeeze. After that, Tonya gave a gift box about the size of her father's hand to Toby.

"This present is for Teal. Take it to her, Toby, so she can open it."

"Pes-ant for Tee! Pes-ant for Tee!" Toby squealed. He sat down right in front of her and clapped his hands. "Ready? Open!" He clapped his hands once again.

This was the first present of hers to open. She was definitely curious to see what it was. It was not the stereo for sure. It might be the gift card. Dad usually put gift cards inside a card or something. He had never taken the time to put them in an actual box and wrap it or anything. She doubted he had changed his gift-wrapping techniques this late in the game.

Teal took off the wrapping paper. The box was generic with nothing on it to give away any hints about what might be inside. She lifted the lid slowly. Inside was something covered in white tissue paper. By now, Toby was nearly sitting on top of her as he watched and waited to see what was inside the box. Teal picked up the item and carefully unwrapped the tissue paper. Usually, when she received stuff covered in tissue paper, it was fragile.

Her father said, "I think it might be upside down. You might have to flip it over. But carefully."

No longer puzzled, Teal looked at him. That meant the item was breakable. Interesting for sure.

It looked like a picture frame. Why would they give her a picture frame? She turned it over.

"Now?" Toby asked, looking over at his mother.

"Yes. You can tell her." Tonya said smiling.

"Baaaaaabbby!" Toby clasped his hands together.

Toby said it just as Teal flipped the picture frame over. It took a moment, but then she realized what Toby meant. Inside the picture frame was a black and white photo with the outline of a baby. In her hand, she was holding an ultrasound picture. Teal seriously did not know what to say. This had been the last thing she had expected. Adopting Toby, okay. Her father getting married, okay. It had never even occurred to her that her father and Tonya might have a child together.

"Are you serious? It's ours? The baby... is ours?" Teal wasn't sure how else to put it. She was excited but was overwhelmed at the same time.

"Yes, the baby is ours." Tonya exclaimed, beaming at Teal's father.

Teal rose from her seat. It seemed appropriate to hug Tonya first, so she did, then she hugged her father. She congratulated them. As she sat down on the floor, Toby walked over to her.

"Budder. Budder. Budder," Toby repeated. He was

going to be a brother.

Teal gave him a high-five. "Yes, you are going to be a big brother!"

Teal could not believe it.

She turned to her father and Tonya who looked so happy together, and now they were adding one more to the family.

It was only after Toby mentioned he was going to be a brother that she realized she was going to be a sister. She would have another sibling. She'd always wanted a brother or sister. She had Toby now, of course, but with this next one, she would be there from the very start.

At that, Toby decided handing out that one gift had been enough for him. He was more interested in opening his own presents. While he did that, Teal decided to get more information. Everyone seemed to be in good spirts, so no time like now. She wanted to know everything, right from the very beginning.

"When is the baby due? Do we know yet?"

"In about six months," her father answered.

"Oh my gosh. Is it a boy or a girl? Do we know?" Suddenly, it seemed like the only important thing was the sex of the baby. Not that it should matter, but right at this moment it did.

Tonya took this question. "They believe we are having a girl."

Teal surprised herself when she actually clapped her hands, just as Toby did when he got excited. It would be awesome. Teal already had a brother, and now she would have a baby sister.

For Christmas, Teal's mother gave her a few smaller things like bath bombs, candles and hand cream along with money for her trip. Without a doubt, this had been the best Christmas she could ever have. No way had she thought this would be possible after seeing her parents split up.

Here she was, though, enjoying Christmas with her parents. Separately, but still, they both seemed genuinely happy, and Teal felt happier than she had in a long time. It felt great.

- 3 -

TEAL NOTICED THAT HER MOTHER had quickly shut the binder in her hands as soon as Teal entered the living room. Her mother had not been spending as much time on the computer, but had been going out a lot more for short intervals "just to grab a coffee." That seemed suspicious. Her mother had never done that before. Teal started wondering if maybe her mother was finally dating someone, and meeting that person at a coffee shop away from the apartment so there would be no chance Teal would run into him or her. That was smart. Wait and see how things go for a while before letting Teal meet the person. Very responsible of her.

"Let me guess. You're going out to grab a coffee." Teal smiled.

Her mother put the binder and a few other items

11

into a laptop bag. "I will be back in a couple of hours. I left money for you and Jackson to order in pizza. I would prefer you stay in tonight."

"We plan to stay in and I am not getting another tattoo anytime soon, Mom. I promise." Teal raised her eyebrows. She figured a decade from now, her mother would still be bringing up the tattoo incident.

After Jackson and Teal had eaten, Teal searched through her backpack to find what she was looking for: a couple of items she'd found in the lock box at the bank.

"Ah. You're finally going to tell me what the box was." Jackson smiled at her.

"I still don't believe it myself. I can't believe Miss Tate left it to me." Teal showed him a photograph of a quaint house situated among others similar in shape, size and color. It appeared to be in a village with old cobblestone-type streets. Already, Teal was enchanted and she hadn't laid eyes on it in reality.

"This is yours?"

"Yep. There are a couple of conditions placed on it, but they're simple. I have to visit the place at least three times and I can't sell it for three years. It doesn't matter how long my visit is, I just have to physically visit it three times. After that, I can do whatever I want with it."

Teal was excited. The house was all hers. She had no

idea if she would sell the place, rent it out, or what, but it seemed exciting that those decisions were ultimately hers to make.

"Sounds great, Teal. But are you going to be able to go visit? Or stay there? I don't mean to make you do a reality check, but the cost of airfare will probably be a least a grand. Doing that three times, plus the money you'll need when you go grocery shopping and that kind of thing. And you have college coming up. Wow. A lot of expenses." Jackson raised his eyebrows in a silent qustion.

Teal stood quietly.

"I'm just saying you may not be able to visit this year."

"Well, I plan on going after graduation. For a month." Teal couldn't help but let out a small squeal after actually saying this. It was exciting just thinking about taking her first plane ride, and to Spain, and to stay in her own house!

"Sounds like a good plan, getting a visit in before college or university starts, but are you going to be able to pay for it?" Doubt was obvious on Jackson's face.

Teal couldn't wait to tell Jackson. The house was not the only thing Miss Tate had left her. "Miss Tate left me money, too. She wanted to make sure I would be able to go visit the house without worrying about paying for the airfare. Good thing you're sitting down, eh, Jackson? You ready for this? She left me ten thousand dollars!" Teal jumped up and down; she was still shocked by the news herself.

"You have to be joking. Why would she leave you money? And a house? You guys weren't even related or anything. She only knew you a couple years."

Teal folded her arms across her chest. Jealous. That was it. He was jealous of the money. He couldn't care less about the house, but the money bothered him.

"I called Dottie after we opened the box at the bank. Apparently, Miss Tate had money. She never married, or had kids. She worked until she was sixty-five and she invested her money here and there. Miss Tate started putting money away when she got her first job at the age of fourteen delivering newspapers. I'm not sure of the exact amount, but she had nearly half a million dollars. She left me what I told you and the rest went to Dottie."

"That's crazy. Good she had money put away, though. She didn't have to worry about becoming one of those cat ladies who also ends up eating wet cat food out of the cans because they don't have enough money to buy proper food." Jackson touched her hand.

"I don't get the money all at once. I get five thousand in May this year, and then twenty-five hundred a year later, and the last chunk a year after that. According to Dottie, Miss Tate figured, with the five thousand she gave me this year, I would be able to spend a couple of weeks at my place in Spain—listen to me, *my* place— and the rest of the money would help pay my tuition for my first semester of school."

"For a grumpy old lady, she sure was smart and turned out to be a pretty amazing person for you. Lucky you."

Teal still wasn't sure by his tone if he was excited for her or not.

"Definitely an amazing lady," she said. "I wish she was still around so I could visit. I know an elderly man moved into her apartment. I think he's alone. Except for a cat, speaking of cats."

This made Jackson smile.

"I saw him walking down the hallway. He was wearing one slipper, the other one was in his hand, and he was using it trying to shoo his cat back into the apartment. I think the cat's name is Oscar. The man has waved to me a few times and I've waved back. I don't know his name yet. Just the cat's name. That's the extent of it."

"For now," Jackson teased.

Teal slapped his leg playfully. She should try to find out the old man's name though.

In a way, she wanted to invite Jackson to go with her on the trip. It would be awesome. Just the two of them on a grand adventure. On the other hand, though, she wanted to make this journey by herself. It almost seemed like a rite of passage or something. In the back of her mind, she was afraid her mother might try to tag along without her knowing. Maybe her mother would arrive in Spain the day after Teal did, say it was only a coincidence she was staying just three blocks from where Teal's house was. Or something like that. She could definitely see her mother attempting to keep her under observation. Teal decided she needed to remain on her best behavior, within reason of course, until she left for the trip. The last thing she wanted to do was give her mother even one single reason why she couldn't be trusted. This would take some effort. Teal hoped she was up to the challenge.

- 4 -

IT HAD BEEN A QUIET Saturday. Just when Teal decided to curl up to write in her journal, her phone went off. A message from Olive.

Hey, Teal, just wondering what you're up to? – O

Teal smiled. She knew Olive better than that. Olive never sent a message to ask what she was doing. What Olive really meant was "Are you doing anything important because I need you for something."

Teal debated.

She was comfortable and didn't want to move. The last couple of days had been great, but they'd tired her out. All the Christmas stuff had been fun, but now she wanted to rest. She wanted to write down some of those good memories to hold onto until a time came

17

when things might not be going so great.

Nothing, was just about to write in my journal. You?-T

Teal should at least see what her friend had to say before she made any decisions.

I'm in trouble.-O

Teal sat up straight. Olive rarely admitted it when things were about to hit the fan, and she *never* did right from the beginning. This was completely out of character for her. Definitely not a good sign.

Teal typed quickly.

Where are you? Are you safe? Are you okay? What's going on?-T

This brought back memories of the time Teal had to go over to Olive's house because Brad, Olive's ex, was trying to break in. It was probably only a second or two until the screen indicated Olive was typing back, but it felt a lot longer than that.

Calm down, Teal. I'm safe. I promise I'm safe. I'm at home. Mom is gone out and no one is here. Just me. I need you to come over. Can you do that?-O

This was weird. How could Olive be in trouble if she was safe at home? No one else was in the house. She had not been attacked or anything. Olive had never lied to her before. Olive had left things out, yes, but she had not lied up front. Therefore, this probably was not some sort of prank. Olive truly did seem upset.

When do you want me to come over?-T
As soon as you can. Like, right now would be great.-O
Okay, on my way.-T

Teal shut the journal and put it away. Her phone beeped again.

Thanks, Teal.-O

She stared at the phone for a full ten seconds. This was not like Olive. It wasn't in her character. Olive rarely said thanks. It wasn't her style.

***

Teal was getting frustrated. She'd been at Olive's house for quite a while now and still had no idea why Olive wanted her there. Olive paced the room. Every so often, she would glance over at Teal, but did not say a word. Finally, Olive tossed a small package at her.

Teal caught it and sat on the bed. She turned the package over to read the English side of it. This was indeed mega serious.

"Oh my god. Seriously?" Teal looked up at Olive.

To her credit, Olive did not look like she was joking

and seemed genuinely upset. It looked like she had tears in her eyes. She stopped pacing.

"That's why I wanted you to come over. I wanted someone. Needed someone. Needed *you* to be with me when I did the test." Olive blew her nose with a tissue from a box beside her bed.

Teal's eyes widened. "Did you already read the instructions?" She felt as though she had to tread extra carefully.

"Yep. Pee on the stick and wait for the stripes. One stripe means you are clear and two stripes mean you have something to fear." Olive walked back and forth once again.

Teal had to stifle a laugh. She had no idea where Olive had heard that saying but it seemed both appropriate and funny at the same time.

"Okay. I'm going to do it. Give me the stick." Olive took the pregnancy test from Teal and went into the bathroom. It seemed to take forever, but in fact, Olive had only been gone for about a minute.

Olive hopped onto the bed. "Now we just have to wait for five minutes." Olive set the timer on her cell phone.

"How bad was it going to the store to buy it? Were you embarrassed?" Teal had managed to enter a tattoo studio and have a tattoo, but did not think she would ever be up to the task of walking into a store to buy a pregnancy test.

"As if. I went to the pharmacy at the Rideau mall and guess what. One of Mom's friends, her name's Holly, was working the counter. No way could I do it. And of course I couldn't wait. I lifted it."

Teal stared at her. What was she talking about? What did she mean, "lifted" it? "What do you mean?"

"You know what I mean. I stole it." Olive shrugged her shoulders like it was no big deal.

"That was stupid. If they'd seen you, they would have arrested you. We're not kids anymore, Olive. If we get into trouble, it's not just a slap on the wrist any- more. We're past that." Teal could not believe what Olive had done.

"I needed to find out. It's not exactly as if I can wait a few weeks or something, right? Anyways, that's over with. I have it. I did the test and now we check." She took in a deep breath.

The timer on Olive's cell chirped.

Olive stood. But did not move.

Teal stayed on the bed.

Olive looked toward the bathroom but stayed where she was.

Teal kept her eyes on Olive and Olive did the same to Teal.

"I can't do it," Olive finally said. "I can't look. You do it. Please? Just look at the test and tell me if there's one stripe or two."

Teal was even more confused now. Olive had had the guts to go into a store and actually steal a pregnancy test, but checking the results of the test was something she wasn't able to do?

Teal couldn't understand why *she* had to be the one to go look at the stupid pee stick. Either way, Olive was going to find out in the next few moments if she was pregnant. Or not. Teal stomped into the bathroom. She wanted this over with, to find out one way or another, so they could move on.

On the counter by the sink lay the pee stick that could change Olive's world and therefore, by default, change Teal's as well. Teal knew that no matter what the stick read, Olive had already drawn her into this. She hesitated, then inched closer. The results were clearly displayed. She could see *them.* There were two dark pink lines. Olive's test was positive. Olive was pregnant. Teal was paralyzed with fear. If she felt this way, she could not even begin to imagine how Olive would feel when she learned the test's result.

She exited the bathroom, at first, too stunned to speak.

"Tell me." Olive's demand was a whisper—as if by

asking quietly, the answer might be the one she wanted to hear. Or if that were to be the case, perhaps there could be time for the results to turn out differently.

Teal still did not trust herself to speak. So instead, she held up two fingers on her right hand, stared at Olive, and nodded yes. She bit her bottom lip.

"It's positive? I'm pregnant?" Olive's face paled.

"Yes." Teal tried to recover from the shock. It wasn't entirely her issue but because of her friendship with Olive, in a way, it partially was.

Olive threw herself onto the bed from where, in between sobs, she murmured "No, not me. No."

Teal was glad she was not in Olive's shoes. Olive's predicament would take time to figure out a solution for. It wasn't a decision to be made lightly. Whatever choice Olive made now would affect the rest of her life. Getting pregnant was something that scared Teal greatly. Although she and Jackson had been together a while, and got along great, they still had not slept together. Jackson had been patient and she appreciated it. Eventually, they would go all the way, but for now, Teal wasn't ready. Teal was still a virgin and Jackson respected that.

On Teal's way home, she made a detour that took her a couple of blocks away from her place. Olive had given her the pregnancy test to get rid of. She didn't want her mother to accidentally find it. Olive needed time to figure things out before she told her. There was no way Teal was going to bring it home and dump it in *their* garbage in case *her* mother found it. *Her* mother would instantly jump to conclusions and it would blow up into a fight. The incident with the tattoo was still fresh in her mother's mind. It would be a while before that episode smoothed over. Teal shouldn't have felt anything when she passed by a trash bin, but for some reason, she did. Nothing she could put a finger on—it just felt like she shouldn't do it. But she did. She threw out the positive pregnancy test.

So now, the only thing Teal could do was support Olive in whatever decision Olive made. She did hope that everything would work out okay for her friend. It would take time, but things always seemed to get back on track for Olive.

- 5 -

JACKSON HANDED TEAL A CUTOUT from a magazine. It was a picture of a tuxedo.

"What do you think? Would this be okay for the prom?" He hadn't gone to his own prom. At that time, they had not been together as a couple very long, so he hadn't bothered to go.

Teal grabbed the cutout. "Looks good," she said as she handed it back.

"We don't have to decide now but we will soon." Jackson raised questioning eyebrows at her.

What was that supposed to mean? They had already discussed it, but still... Teal was fine with the prom itself. She could handle that. What she wasn't sure of was the part that generally happened *after* prom. She realized it was only natural to lose your virginity eventually and

Jackson was her first actual relationship.

Jackson shoved the paper into his back pocket. "Teal. The color. We have to decide on the color soon because when I go and put a hold on the suit, they're going to ask me. If we don't decide soon, I'll end up with whatever's left over so there's a good chance we won't match."

Okay, maybe he hadn't been thinking of their having sex together for the first time. On the other hand, maybe he had and then saw Teal's reaction so responded with this matching color thing.

"Yes, okay, soon. We'll figure out the color scheme soon. I'm undecided." Teal was telling him the truth. She was trying to make a choice between purple and turquoise as their color scheme. Too many choices to worry about right now. She was also unsure of what prom night might hold in store for them after the dance was over. Jackson and Teal had talked about intimacy in general on several occasions. Jackson wasn't a virgin. In a way, she'd been shocked when she found out, but at the same time, she would have been shocked if he had been. As if that made any sense at all. About a year before he met Teal, Jackson had dated a girl for a couple of months. One night, after a few too many drinks, they had slept together. It hadn't been her first time, but it had been his. A week later, she had broken it off with him and hadn't said why. According to Jackson, they didn't get along that well to begin with, so it was for the best.

The prom was still a few months away. More time to think of how she felt about Jackson and if she was ready for this next step. But right now, above everything else, she needed to figure out what color of dress she would be wearing.

- 6 -

OLIVE'S EYES PLEADED. SHE NEEDED him right now. They had to figure things out. They had to figure out *the situation* they were currently in together. It was not only her responsibility, but his, too. It was not as though she'd managed to get pregnant on her own or anything. But that was the way he was behaving.

"I'm not lying, Brad. I took the test a couple days ago. It came out positive."

"So. What do you want from me?" Brad spat out the words. "What do you want me to do about it?"

Olive knew he would not be happy with the news but she hadn't pictured the discussion going quite like this.

"I want us to talk about it. It's a decision we have to make together." Olive continued to fold his laundry.

"I think this is your problem. Not mine." He turned away from her.

Olive stopped.

"*We* slept together. *We* got pregnant. Therefore, it is a *we* problem." Surely, he was not so ignorant that he could not see that.

"The way I see it, *you* had sex with someone and got pregnant, so it's a *you* problem." Brad stood with his hands on his hips. He definitely looked upset.

"I didn't have sex with *someone*. I had sex with *you*, Brad. Just you, and deep down you know that. It's yours, Brad. Ignoring this is not going to help." Olive stood her ground and was secretly quite impressed with herself.

He stood quietly for a moment. Then, without warning, he lunged forward to slap her hard across the face. She fell to the floor. Her left cheek felt on fire.

"Liar! Get out now!" he hollered.

She could not believe it. He had hit her. She was stunned. She grabbed her bag and ran out the door.

Olive didn't know where to go. She didn't want to hang around outside in case Brad decided to come after her. She didn't want to be anywhere near him. That was the last thing she wanted and needed right now. There was no way she could go home like this. She was too upset. She needed a few hours to calm down before she even thought of going home. It was too bad she didn't have a cool father like Teal did. She hadn't talked to her own father in years.

Teal. She could go to Teal's. She would beg her not to say anything to anyone. She could handle this. Brad had just been a little upset with her. That's all. It was to be expected. She'd had a few days to process the news of the pregnancy, and this was the first he'd heard of it. Everything would be fine once he'd had time to calm down and think things through. That was all. There really wasn't a choice. She had to wait things out. No big deal really. Right? She wiped tears away, adjusted her bag and immediately felt more in control. Her best bet was to head for Teal's place. Best not to let Teal know she was on her way in case Teal wasn't home, or was busy. No way could she handle that. Best to show up unannounced and take things from there. She kept her fingers crossed as she walked to Teal's. It felt like everyone was staring at her. She tried to stop her tears, but her system wouldn't listen.

***

Teal heard the knock at their apartment door. She smiled. It was probably Jackson, a surprise visit, which she always welcomed. Her smile faded away quickly when she saw Olive standing there. Olive was a mess, her hair was sticking out in places and Teal could not even see her face clearly. She could tell her best friend had been crying. Still was, in fact, but trying to cover it up.

Right now, words didn't matter. Teal did the first thing that came to mind. She wrapped her arms around her friend.

"Shhh. It's going to be okay. Whatever it is, it will be okay." Teal held onto her.

Arm across Olive's shoulder, Teal guided her to the couch and sat her down. Teal tried to straighten Olive's hair to get it away from her face, but Olive flinched. It took a couple of tries before Teal realized Olive was hiding something.

"Oh my gosh. Did Brad do that? Did he hit you?" Teal could detect a slight swelling on Olive's face.

"I told him I was pregnant, and he got upset," Olive sobbed. "But he'll calm down, and then we can talk. He'll be more reasonable then."

This time Olive did not pull back when Teal moved the hair away from her face. Olive's cheek had already started to bruise, and her left eye was swollen.

"I'll be right back. I'll go get some ice to put on that."

As Teal was wrapping the ice cubes in a cloth, she heard the apartment door shut.

"Olive. What happened? Were you robbed?" Teal's mother rushed over.

Teal handed Olive the ice to put on her face before

shaking her head, no, to her mother.

Her mother's expression was one of confusion. Teal kept quiet and hoped someone else would say something. She really had no idea what to say or do right at that moment.

"It was Brad, wasn't it?"

For a moment, it looked like her mother was going to continue, maybe even start with a big lecture on the good-for-nothing Brad, but Teal was grateful that her mother had managed to stop herself. The last thing Olive needed right now was a lecture, especially from her best friend's mother.

Teal and her mother managed to get Olive cleaned up. Olive sipped at a hot apple cider. She had not said much but that was okay.

When Olive's cell phone went off, Teal locked eyes with Olive.

"If it's him, don't answer back," Teal's mom advised. "No matter what he says, don't answer him back."

Olive picked up her cell phone and checked the message. It was from Brad.

This is your entire fault, Olive. How could you let this happen?-B

Teal expected Olive to answer back the moment her mother left the living room to go to the kitchen, but she didn't. Instead, she turned the phone to silent mode and put it back in her purse.

Olive looked up at Teal as she took the last sip of her cider.

"Would it be okay if I spent the night here?" Olive's eyes pleaded.

Teal was caught off guard. It had been quite a while since the two of them had had a sleepover.

"Of course. I'll get Mom call your place to save you having to." Teal smiled as she sat beside Olive on the couch. "How about we order in Chinese food, as well? That sound good?"

She saw the beginnings of a small smile on Olive's lips. "Chinese food and a sleepover sounds really good right now. Thanks."

They touched hands.

***

It was a quiet evening. Olive and Teal ordered in Chinese food and decided to watch all four of the *Scream* movies. Those were among Olive's all-time favorites and Teal didn't mind them. Olive didn't say much, but that was okay. The fact that she ate and let out a small laugh every so often during the first movie was enough. A couple of times, Olive gingerly touched her cheek. It broke Teal's heart to watch this happening, but maybe this incident would be enough for

Olive to leave Brad for good.

As the second movie started, Teal got a text message. She figured it might be from Jackson. It wasn't. It was from her mother.

> Just wanted to give you a head's up that I have spoken to Olive's mom about what happened. She has either already called or will be calling the police on Brad. He was supposed to keep out of trouble because he is still out on bail from when he tried to break into Olive's place. It will just be a matter of time before Brad is picked up and arrested once again.-M

Teal stared at the phone. She didn't know what to say. She was on her mother's side, of course. Brad hadn't followed the rules, and there were consequences for not following rules. But she didn't want Olive to get upset all over again.

Maybe it would be best for Teal to wait until morning to say anything to her. That way there was at least a chance Olive might get some sleep. If she told her now, they'd both be up all night discussing everything.

***

At the table the next morning, Olive brought up the incident first. Teal was surprised but grateful as well. It would make things easier.

"I took a look in the mirror and I look like crap." Olive accentuated this by gently touching her cheek.

"It's even worse than I looked and felt yesterday."

"That's how it usually goes. When you get hurt, it feels worse for the next couple of days. It should feel better soon. Are you going to go back to him for more?" Teal asked this as she stood up to take the dishes to rinse them off in the sink.

If looks could kill, Teal would be dead right now. Olive looked like she was ready to pounce.

Teal stayed at the sink and took her sweet time rinsing the dishes off.

"Are you saying this is my fault?" Olive asked in a raised voice.

"I didn't say that. What I meant was that he has treated you badly before. He cheated on you. He tried to break into your house. And other stuff. Now he has physically abused you. He slapped you, Olive." Teal turned to look at her friend.

Olive made no comment and Teal could not read her face.

"I didn't want to tell you last night, but your mom knows what happened and called the police. Brad is back in jail and they will not let him out for at least a couple days. Maybe even a week. He'll be in there until some of his charges go to court." Teal inched her way toward Olive.

"I figured as much," Olive said as she helped load

the dishes into the dishwasher.

"How did you know?"

Olive's smile was more of a smirk. "Easy. Your mother was too calm about the whole thing. I figured the minute we headed to your room to watch the movies, she'd be on the phone to my mom and it would go from there. I was right. I'm actually surprised that my mom didn't show up to give me trouble for being with him and drag me home. I'm glad she didn't. It was good to spend a nice quiet evening with you. No drama. Just like we used to." Then the tears fell freely.

Teal put her arms around her.

- 7 -

TEAL LOOKED OVER AT THE message on her phone's screen. She was supposed to go over to her father's place later on in the afternoon. Maybe plans had changed or something. The message read:

It's important. Please call me when you get the chance.-Dad

That did not sound good. She closed her journal and turned down the radio before she dialed his number.

"Dad. I got your message. What is going on?"

"It's Tonya. She's at the hospital. Her water leaked and it's too early for the baby to be born yet." Dad's voice sounded weird.

"Oh my gosh. What does this mean? What can we do?" Instantly, Teal was on her feet pacing her bedroom, but after two fast turns, she stopped. All she had accomplished was to make herself physically dizzy on top of being dizzy with worry.

"Well, like I said, right now we're at the hospital. They have her comfortable and lying in a bed. I have Toby with me. If you don't have any plans, it would be great if you could come here. We're at the Civic. This is where her doctor delivers out of the obstetrical unit. Just ask at the information desk how to get here. I can't be chasing Toby around and trying to figure out what's going on with Tonya at the same time. Of course, the poor little guy doesn't understand what's going on, so he's getting upset. I'm sure he'd love to see you."

He did not need to plead. Of course, she'd go help. After all, Toby was her step-brother and she would soon have a sister. She had responsibilities now. Besides, this was an emergency, a *family* emergency.

"Of course. I'll be there as fast as I can, Dad. I'll text you when I'm close so you can tell me how to get to the information desk. Hang in there, Dad. Love you."

"Are you sure you don't mind? I did talk to your mother and she's willing to help out, as well." He didn't sound convinced.

"I'm on my way, Dad." She hung up the phone. She said goodbye to Olive as she left for the hospital.

***

As Teal entered the hospital room, she stopped for a moment. Toby was sitting beside Tonya on the right side of the bed, and was holding her hand. On the left, Dad was holding Tonya's other hand and he looked upset. Not that Teal could blame him. She herself had never seen Tonya like that. It tugged at her heart. It was amazing how, over time, things could change so completely. A couple of years earlier, when she'd met this same woman, she'd wanted nothing to do with her. Teal had feared this woman would try and take her father away from her.

Teal hugged her father first.

As soon as Toby spotted her, he hopped off the bed and came running around the end of the bed toward her. "Teeeeeeeeeeeeeeeeeeeeeeee!" he squealed.

Teal loved how he got all excited to see her, and the way he said her name gave her goosebumps. Not that she would ever tell her father or Tonya that.

She picked Toby up, swung him around, set him back down and gave him a high-five.

As Toby crawled back up onto his mother's hospital bed, Teal approached Tonya and placed her hand on her shoulder. Teal didn't want to risk a hug because she wasn't sure if Tonya was in pain or not. This kind of scenario was all new to Teal.

"How are you doing? Are you in any pain?"

Tonya sat up straighter and clasped her hands protectively over her abdomen.

"They gave me something for the pain. I'm comfortable. We're just worried about the baby. I'm only thirty-two weeks along. I still have another eight weeks to go before Peanut is due to arrive." Tonya teared up and reached for a tissue.

Despite the seriousness of the situation, Teal half smiled at Tonya's use of the name "Peanut." Once, Teal had accidentally called her sibling-to-be that, and it had stuck. That's what everyone was currently calling the baby.

Two doctors walked in.

"We need a moment to speak with the two of you," the taller one said.

Teal glanced at her father and nodded. Then she turned to her step-brother. "Toby? Do you want to go with me to get a treat?"

"Yes, Teeee." Toby nearly fell off the hospital bed as he tried to jump into her arms. The offer of a treat, with all its mystery, worked like a charm every time.

"Thanks, Teal." Her father patted her shoulder.

***

Toby sat beside her on the cafeteria bench. Smarties were strewn all over the table and the box was empty. He had one in his mouth as he played with the others.

He was nice and quiet right now, and she let him be so she could enjoy it while it lasted. She was very worried about Tonya and the baby. Peanut needed more time in order to be healthy. What were the chances of the baby being okay if it was born in the next few days?

It was somewhat ironic when Teal thought about it. Here was Tonya, super happy about being a mother again but having complications. Then there was Olive, having been dealt an unplanned pregnancy with an abusive boyfriend.

Teal pulled herself out of her concerned thoughts. She needed to focus on Toby now. Toby, her sweet step-brother, who had been sorting his Smarties into different piles with each color in its own pile. She was impressed so decided to take a picture and send it to her father.

***

Somehow, Teal managed to keep Toby busy for over an hour before heading back to the room. She hoped the doctors were gone, and her parents had more information as to what the next steps would be for Peanut. Teal caught herself referring to her father and Tonya as her parents. It felt good.

No matter what, her father always tried to put on a smile, so his smile on their return didn't necessarily mean they'd received good news.

"There's my smart man." Her father gave Toby a high-five.

Teal was pleased. Obviously, her father had received the photo of Toby and the Smarties. After the high-five, Toby climbed onto the bed beside his mother.

Tonya put her arm around Toby before clearing her throat. "The plan, as of now, is to keep me here for a week to help keep the baby inside for as long as possible. If things are okay after that, and there are no more symptoms of the baby coming early, I will be able to go home. But will have to be on bed rest." Tonya shrugged her shoulders.

Teal had a good idea but wasn't entirely sure, so she asked. "What does bed rest mean?"

Her father was the one who replied. "It means exactly that. Tonya will have to stay in bed and rest. She won't be able to take Toby out to the park, run errands or anything like that. If she does, it might trigger an early labor, which we don't want. The longer she can keep the baby inside, the better. Best until she's at least thirty-eight weeks."

"Yikes. That's going to be hard. Are you going to be able to take some time off work, Dad?"

"I can take some time but not too much because I want to be able to be with Tonya and the baby after it's born." Teal's father scratched his head then continued to check stuff on his phone.

Teal knew she'd be expected to help but that was okay. It would be good, though, if she had control of just how much help they'd expect of her and when.

"Dad?"

Her father looked up from his cell phone.

"I can watch Toby for a couple of hours once or twice during the week so you can go run errands, or whatever needs to be done. I'll come over on Sundays, too. Maybe spend the day helping out?"

Tonya cut in. "It would be great if you could throw in a load or two of laundry a week. I don't trust your father." She smiled over at him. "Remember that time you bleached all my new clothes? Who adds bleach to black clothes?"

"Sure," said Teal. "I can do cleaning, throw in a laundry, do dishes, play with Toby." She smiled at her little brother. "Especially play with Toby. And I can take him out so he isn't climbing the walls too much."

"Thanks, honey. It means a lot to me that we can count on you." Her father's hug felt good. The extra time spent helping out with Toby would take time away from schoolwork, and Jackson, but it would work out. Besides, maybe Jackson would go with her to her father's a couple of times and take Toby out with her.

- 8 -

AS SOON AS OLIVE WALKED into the living room, she knew something had happened. The air felt as though her mother had been lurking in ambush. Olive knew from experience this was definitely not a good sign so she sat down on the edge of the couch.

Her mother asked right up front. "When was the exact last time you had any contact with Brad?"

If Brad were the topic, there might be a chance that Olive, herself, wasn't in trouble. Behind her back, she crossed the fingers of both hands, hoping this would be the case.

"The last time I saw him was the day he hit me." Olive made sure her eyes met her mother's so her mother would know she was telling the truth.

"What about the last time you spoke on the phone?

Or through text? Or whatever, since that day?" Her mother had both hands on her hips now, and towered over her. Absolutely definitely not a good sign. This always meant things would be taking a turn for the even worse. Olive still wasn't sure exactly why her mother was upset.

"Three days after I spent the night at Teal's, he sent me a text saying he loved me, he was sorry and that it wouldn't happen again. He wanted to know if I could forgive him. And he asked me to visit him in jail up at Innes. Said he had put my name on the visitors' list and everything already." Olive looked down at the floor. She hadn't lied, but had no idea what was going on so was even less confident about making direct eye contact with her mother.

"And how did you reply?" her mother breathed out slowly.

"I sent one text message back saying it was over and not to contact me again. That was it. Just the one message."

"Nothing else to add?"

"Just what I said. You don't believe me, do you?" Olive took the cell phone out of her purse and held it up at arm's length. "Check if you want. They're there. All the messages from him. You can see for yourself I haven't answered a single one!"

Her mother made no move to take the phone so Olive tossed it onto the couch beside her.

"Zero phone calls, visits or texts since the night he hit you? That's the truth?"

Olive closed her eyes. She wanted to say something about the fact that her mother never seemed to believe her, but thought it best she tread carefully.

"Yes. I swear." Olive unclenched her hands.

"Well, guess what Brad did today?"

Olive sat up straight. What could he do from jail? Or maybe they'd let him out and he'd come to the house?

"What are you talking about, Mom? What did he do? I swear I had nothing to do with it." She didn't know how else to convince her mother. She was telling the truth.

"I definitely think you are wrong this time, Olive."

Olive raised her eyebrows. What story was Brad trying to make up now? She didn't know what to say.

"He used the payphone at Innes. Inmates are allowed to do that, you know, and he called here. He asked to speak to you and, of course, I said no. He wanted to talk to you because he told me that he had been doing some thinking and has come up with a few potential names for the baby." Her voice was much louder now.

"Shit," was all Olive managed to say. She wasn't sure

if she should remain seated on the couch or stand up in case she had to run or something. She was both embarrassed and scared at the same time. She stood.

"So it's true. You are pregnant. I don't need to ask how it happened. Tell me you were using something." Her mother quietly sank onto the couch.

Good sign. This meant things were less likely to get heated.

"Of course, Brad and I used something. It just happened. I don't know why but it did. You don't think I'm smart enough to think? I know I'm too young." Olive sat down again, but as far away from her mother as she could.

"Don't raise your voice at me and don't use his name. You know I can't stand him. I told you before he was up to no good and he will always hold you back. You deserve so much better, Olive."

Olive looked up. It wasn't often her mother paid her a compliment.

"Do you know how far along you are?"

"I think about five or six weeks at the most. I missed my period and a week later, I took the test. I still can't believe it."

"What are you going to do? I can't make the decision for you. It's yours to make. But I *will* try to be supportive."

"I don't know. How much time do I have to figure things out?" Olive asked. This was overwhelming. Her mother had been eighteen when she'd had Olive.

Her mother shrugged. "I'm not a hundred percent sure but at the most maybe six weeks," she offered.

"That's good. I mean, that's good that I have some time to think about it. I really have no idea what I'm going to do. None of the options seems good." Olive sank deeper into the couch. She wished she could disappear into it.

Her mother patted Olive's knee. "I just don't want to lose you. You're all that I have in this world. You have your whole life ahead of you."

Somehow, this made Olive feel somewhat better.

- 9 -

TEAL CHECKED THE PHONE. IT was Olive.

"Hey what's up?"

"My mom knows I am pregnant!"

"You told her? Wow."

"No. I would never have told her. It was Brad. He called here because he wanted to speak to me so we could talk about possible names for our baby."

"You are joking."

"I wish I was, but I am not. I wasn't home so obviously he left that message with my mother. I can't believe he's such a prick."

"Okay, so now what? Are you allowed to leave the house? Is she burning your stuff? Is she going down to the jail to talk some business with Brad? What's going on?" Teal fired question after question at her.

"No. Mom's handling it okay. I still don't know what I'm doing. Mom hasn't mentioned that I was grounded or anything, but if you don't hear from me for a bit, then you'll know she changed her mind."

"Well, at least you don't have to keep it a secret from her anymore." Teal offered. She honestly wasn't sure what else there was to say. "What are you going to do next?" Olive's situation was time sensitive.

"Make an appointment with my doctor and go from there. Maybe she can give me more information on the different options. I know there's stuff out all over the Internet, but this is not something to mess around with."

Teal giggled.

"What's so funny, Teal? Seriously, there's nothing funny going on."

"You, being serious. It's not like you at all. It will take getting used to."

"I don't have a choice, do I? This isn't some small thing. It's huge and can change things for me for the rest of my life. Plus, it's not as if I can just sit and wait for months to figure this one out. It has to be soon."

"I'll come with you to your doctor's appointment if you want me to," Teal offered.

"That would be great. I'll let you know when the appointment is. Thanks."

***

An hour later, Teal received Olive's text with the date and time of the appointment. Olive was giving herself time to think things over. Impressive. Teal wondered if Olive's mother would be invited to come with them.

- 10 -

AS TEAL LOCKED HER APARTMENT door, the next-door neighbor opened his. It looked like he was heading out. Teal nodded in the direction of the elderly man with the cat named Oscar.

She took the initiative. "Morning, Mister. How are you?"

At first, he didn't say anything, but as she put her keys away in her bag, he answered. "I'm okay thanks."

Before she could say anything else, he was walking fast past her, right out of the apartment building. Strange, but it was a start. Maybe they would strike up a conversation over the next couple of months.

She headed to her father's place.

Tonya had only three weeks and a couple of days left until the baby was born. This was good. Everything seemed to be going smoothly. If the baby could wait a little longer, they would be out of the woods. Teal dumped all the clean clothes out of the laundry basket and onto the bed to fold them. She was nearly half done when Toby ran into the room.

"Tee. Candy!" Toby said, giving her his best but-I'm-so-cute smile. It was Teal's own fault. A couple weeks ago, she had bought a box of Fruit by the Foot and Toby had fallen in love with them. The candy was like Play-Doh. It could be molded, and you could eat it as well.

They were waiting for Olive and then the three of them were going to the park for a while to give Tonya a break.

Teal's father was at work and wouldn't be back any time soon. An elderly woman, Stella, on the ground floor of one of the buildings he supervised, had forgotten she was cooking something on the stove when she went to her friend Pippy's three doors down and asked to visit and have tea.

Stella and Pippy had just sat down to enjoy their tea when the building's fire alarm went off. It wasn't until after the fire department had arrived and gone into the apartment to put out the fire that she realized it was all happening in her apartment. It was Teal's father's job to figure out everything that needed to be done.

Teal would have her cell phone on in case Tonya

needed anything, and the park was only a fifteen-minute walk from the apartment.

A knock sounded at the door. When Teal looked through the peephole, Olive stuck out her tongue.

Laughing, Teal opened the door and as soon as Toby saw Olive, he chanted, "Live, Live, Live."

"Give me a high-five, Toby!"

Toby slapped twice, once on each hand.

"Let's head out," Teal said, then called to Tonya. "We're leaving now."

"Okay. Thanks." Tonya yelled back.

***

At the park, Toby sat on the swing for a bit then decided he wanted to play in the sand and make things with his blue shovel and bucket and his molds. Olive and Teal sat with him and mindlessly dug or drew X's and O's in the sand.

"How are you really doing?" Teal asked, as she looked Olive directly in the eye.

"Could be better. Plus, the run-in with Brad's mother, Marlene, kind of shook Mom up."

"What? I didn't know about that." Teal was genuinely surprised this had somehow gotten past her.

"Seriously,? You didn't know?"

"Mom never said anything." Teal found it hard to believe that her mother had purposely held something back. Her mother loved to take ordinary situations and use them as a life lessons for Teal. Her mother never missed an opportunity.

"Yikes. Guess my mom is keeping it on the down low big time if she didn't mention it to yours. A good thing, I guess. The less people know, the better. I have enough to deal with. I don't need any fuel added to the fire. As they say."

"Come on. So what happened?"

Clap. Clap. Clap. Toby was proud. "It's a cassile!" he exclaimed.

"It's absolutely beautiful," Teal told him quickly and patted his head before turning back to Olive. The conversation continued.

"Mom was doing groceries, minding her own business, then all of a sudden, she feels a tap on her left shoulder. She turns around and it's Marlene. Mom knows who Marlene is, of course, so she says 'Hi.'

"Then Marlene puts her hands on her hips and starts telling Mom that I told lies about my pregnancy. How, that even if I *was* pregnant, we'd never know who the baby daddy was because of all the men I've dated. That Mom needs to keep me away from her Brad."

Teal put her hand over her mouth to try to suppress her giggle, but it didn't work very well. "So did your mom smack her across the face?"

This brought a smile to Olive's worried face.

Beside them, Toby began to flatten his castles with a few of the cars he'd brought along with him.

"She told me she felt like it but managed to control herself." A full smile from Olive now. "She told Marlene to mind her own damn business and if she ever spoke to her like that again she would personally guarantee there would *not* be another run-in. Ever. "

"That's crazy. Hopefully that family leaves you alone."

After a couple more sandcastles, Toby lost interest and wanted to go on the swing. Teal and Olive pushed him back and forth and continued to chat.

"How are things between you and Jackson?" Olive asked.

Teal couldn't help but blush. She still couldn't believe someone would be interested in her. Yet they were still together. "Still going well. We're good." Teal almost went on about what a great guy he was but that would have made Olive flinch for sure. "So you're hanging in there? How *are* things between you and your mom? Tell me the truth."

For a moment, Olive didn't say anytyhing. She pushed Toby a couple more times, then answered. "It's complicated. My emotions are all over the place. Some-times Mom seems supportive and other times, when she looks at me, I can see disappointment all over her face, and it hurts. It really hurts. More than Brad ever hurt me. I don't know if that makes any sense to you at all. It's hard." Olive looked like she was about to cry.

"It's hard for your mom, as well. " Teal tried to give Olive a winning smile but she must not have been convincing because Olive didn't acknowledge it. "Things'll get back on track. It takes time."

"Actually, I feel a little off right now. Can we go back to Toby's place?"

"Sure. It's been nearly two hours. We must have worn Toby out at least a little bit. When we get in, we can always pop in one of his fave movies, make popcorn and guaranteed, he'll be asleep fifteen minutes into the movie."

Teal loaded all the sandbox toys into the bag.

- 11 -

BACK AT HER FATHER'S APARTMENT, Teal and Olive heard a weird noise. Teal looked at Olive quickly and ran to Tonya's bedroom. Tonya had curled herself up, almost into a ball. She let out a moan. Olive rushed to her side.

Tonya's eyes met with hers. She smiled weakly.

"What's going on? Are you okay?" Teal asked, panicked.

"I'm pretty sure it's time. My water broke." Tonya looked around at the wet mess all over the bed.

"You serious. Why didn't you call me?" Teal tried to help Tonya move out of the wet zone of the mattress to a drier area.

"I was going to but as I reached for my cell phone, I accidentally knocked it off my bed." Tonya pointed to

58

the floor on the right side of the bed.

Teal reached down and picked up the phone. She used Tonya's thumb to unlock it, scrolled the contacts and found her father's number, then called. As his phone started ringing, she put the phone on speaker so she could multi-task. The last thing she needed was the baby to pop out right here. That was not happening! Luckily, on top of Tonya's diaper bag, still packed since she'd been at the hospital before, was an outfit for Tonya to wear. Teal quickly grabbed it and handed it to Tonya who stood up and started pacing, her face wincing. Teal's father still hadn't answered his phone. No doubt, things were even worse at the fire site than he had originally thought.

After that contraction passed, Tonya sat on the bed again to take her clothes off and put on the dry ones. Teal turned away and fiddled with the diaper bag, adjusting things. She didn't want to embarrass Tonya by watching her dress, but she didn't feel right leaving her in the bedroom alone in case she fell or something.

A couple minutes later Tonya was dressed, Teal had the diaper bag, and they were in the living room.

Olive looked nervous. "Is your dad on his way?"

"He's not answering. And I don't think it's a good idea to wait. I think we should go to the hospital."

"Okay... And just how are you getting there? What

about Toby?"

"Oh," said Teal. It was a good question.

"Okay. I know. Teal? You go to the hospital with Tonya and I'll stay here and watch Toby. If you want, I can keep trying to reach your dad."

"Awesome. That would be great. That will save us the worry about Toby. Now I just need to figure out how to get her to the hospital."

Teal glanced over at Tonya who had the car keys in her hand and was heading for the door.

"I've only driven a couple of times," Teal said, "but I do have my G1. The hospital's not super far. I could give it a shot."

"Not happening." Tonya hunched over with another contraction. "Thanks, Olive. You're a dear. We'll be fine. Please don't worry. I'll call later with an update."

Tonya hugged Toby who then took her hand as though he expected to be going with her. Tonya leaned down to explain that he had to stay home and wait for his little sister or brother to show up. That she needed to go to the hospital for that to happen. Once Toby heard the word hospital, he settled down and went back to the living room to look for a movie that he and Olive could watch.

When Teal hugged Olive goodby, she whispered a thank you then she and Tonya headed out.

The drive to the hospital was one of the worst rides Teal had ever experienced. Tonya would drive normally for a bit and then a contraction would take hold and it was a struggle. Sometimes she would start speeding up or brake too fast and she even ran a stop sign. Finally, after nearly forty minutes, they arrived at the hospital, and in one piece. Miraculously, a security guard had been roaming around the parking lot and helped them nab a parking spot within a short time. At the entrance door, Teal grabbed a wheelchair and helped Tonya get into it. She left the diaper bag in the trunk along with the suitcase. She figured they were not needed right away.

Tonya instructed her to the maternity ward. The woman at the desk was super nice. Teal appreciated this as she had no idea what she was doing. After the receptionist informed them that Tonya was in labor, as if that wasn't obvious, Teal thought it best to answer when a question was asked as it didn't seem like Tonya was up to the task.

Finally, once Tonya was helped into a gown and settled in a delivery room, Teal was able to relax. She tried calling her father again, but still couldn't get through. She sent Olive a text letting her know they had made it to the hospital and thanked her again for watching Toby.

Olive replied with a quick "Welcome."

A nurse came into the room, announced that her name was Gillian, and that she had just started her shift. Teal stayed by Tonya's side but felt absolutely useless. There wasn't any point in calling her father every thirty seconds, either. She would keep trying but she needed to be there for Tonya. Besides, Olive was continuing to try to get through to him. Teal's job right now was to make sure Tonya was as comfortable as she could possibly be.

Teal put her hand on the bed near Tonya. "Is there anything I can do to help?"

Tonya grabbed her hand and squeezed it.

"Just your being here is a big help."

The nurse smiled at them. "It's nice your daughter's here to witness the birth of her sibling. A rare but exciting opportunity indeed."

Tonya and Teal locked eyes and smiled. Neither bothered to correct the nurse. It didn't matter now. By now, it didn't matter at all.

- 12 -

IT WAS JUST BEFORE SHE received Teal's text letting her know they'd arrived at the hospital when she felt it: a sharp pain in her lower abdomen.

She was on the couch with Toby but there was still room to stretch out. That helped a bit. Maybe it was stress or something, so it was best to relax. The movie *Moana* was playing. This was good. Toby would be distracted—quiet—for the next while. Maybe he would even fall asleep. As long as he was quiet, all would be good. Right now, she had to get herself comfortable.

To take her mind off her discomfort, she would try once again to reach Teal's father. No luck.

Toby was a sweet kid. He really was. Until recently, she had never even thought of having kids or not having kids. It was a topic that hadn't crossed her mind.

To be fair, though, she was too young. Seeing Toby and spending time with him, as well as the whole pregnancy thing, had really slammed into her. The thought was there constantly now. Plus, there was a huge urgency for her to make a decision. No matter what she thought about her situation, when it came down to the choices, she didn't like any of them. So how then was she supposed to be confident that she would make the right decision? How was she supposed to live with that decision? She already knew the answer to her own question. No matter the decision, she would have to live with it the rest of her life. And it would haunt her.

***

Teal couldn't help but glance over at the entrance to the delivery room every so often. Where was her father? Of course he had the emergency at work but this was important, too. More so. There must be someone who could take over for a while so he could come to the hospital. Teal had never seen Tonya angry and she wanted to keep it that way if she had anything to do with it.

"Where's your dad?" Tonya asked as another contraction hit.

"He's on his way." Teal lied without hesitation, thinking if she kept Tonya calm, everything would work out fine.

"As soon as this contraction is over," said Gillian, the nurse, who was almost constantly at Tonya's bedside, "I'm going to check again to see how far you're dilated."

Tonya and Teal's eyes locked, then Teal left the room to give Tonya and Gillian privacy for a moment.

She called back. "I'll call him again right now, Tonya. Just try to relax, okay?"

Then at last, her father's voice.

Outside the hospital room, Teal tapped her foot impatiently. "Where are you? Are you on your way?"

"Teal! No, I'm not off work yet. I don't get off until..." He paused. " What's going on? Is everything okay?"

"Dad! Don't you ever check your messages? Didn't Olive talk to you? Get to the hospital. Now!" As people passed by, they glanced at her with raised eyebrows. Teal didn't care.

"Hospital? Oh my gosh." Her father's voice rose. "It's Tonya? She's having the baby?"

"Yes. Took you long enough to catch on. Her water broke a while ago. They're checking her dilation again. Whatever that means. That's what the nurse said, anyway. You need to be here. That's all I know."

"I am on my way. Tell her not to move. To wait for me."

Teal laughed. Where was Tonya going to go at this stage?

"Sure, Dad. I'll tell her. And bring me a coffee or something. Bring me anything. Maybe you should bring something for yourself, too. This isn't easy. Love ya, bye."

Teal hung up before her father could ask any more questions. Then she made a quick call to her mother to let her know where she was, and not to expect her home any time soon. After Tonya had the baby, she would want to stay for a bit.

Next on the list was Olive, but there was no response to Teal's text.

What was Olive's problem, now? She'd been left with only a couple responsibilities. All she had to do was, one, watch Toby, who was probably asleep. And two, get hold of Teal's father, which she had obviously not done. It wasn't as if Teal ever asked a whole lot of Olive—ever. Today was different, though. She had counted on Olive. But maybe Olive had fallen asleep on the couch, cuddled with Toby, while watching a movie, as Teal often did herself. That was possible. She would try again later.

***

Back in the hospital room, Teal met with Tonya's questioning face. "He'd better be on his way."

Teal had to smile. She had never seen this side of Tonya before. She rather liked it. "Yeah. He is. No worries. He'll be here. Just do what they tell you."

While Teal had been out of the room making phone calls, the nurse had checked Tonya. They were nearly there. It was almost time to push. So far, Tonya had refused to take anything for the pain, but the pain seemed to be getting worse, though, and the baby was still inside. How much longer could Tonya hold out?

"You sure you don't want anything for the pain?" Gillian asked Tonya.

Tonya stared at her.

"I'm only asking because soon it will be time to start pushing. I thought I'd ask now because soon, even if you want pain medication, it will be too late. I have to keep asking."

"I'm fine. It doesn't tickle but I think I'll be okay."

Teal admired her for saying no to pain medication. As she watched Tonya, she'd already decided that when the time came for *her* to have kids, she would *definitely* take pain medication. As far as she knew, no special awards were given out to women who had all-natural births.

"Uh oh," Tonya said, looking at Teal.

"What's wrong?"

Gillian rushed to Tonya's side.

"Tell me. What's going on?" Gillian insisted.

"I feel like I have to push, but he isn't here yet. He's

going to miss the whole damn thing!"

When Tonya squeezed her fingers into a fist, Teal wondered if this was because her father wasn't there yet, or if the pain had worsened. Either way, it wasn't a good sign.

Struggling, Tonya moved around on the bed, Teal guessed it was to make herself feel more comfortable.

A commotion in the hall made all three of them turn toward the door. Teal's father flew into the room, almost tripping over his own feet, but miracuously not spilling his tray of three Tim Horton's Iced Capps.

A half hour later, Teal's baby sister arrived weighing five pounds, eleven ounces. Not bad considering she was a few weeks early. Teal couldn't believe how beautiful she was.

Now that her father was there, it was time to find out what was up with Olive. She couldn't wait to tell her they'd named the baby Violet Teal Flint. The "Teal" part, after her.

- 13 -

AS GENTLY AS SHE COULD, Olive slid Toby off her and onto the couch. He stayed asleep. Good. She didn't have to worry about him for the moment. She slipped a blanket over him.

She had thought for sure after she'd taken something for the pain in her abdomen, that it would have gone away, but it was being persistent.

After propping a cushion in front of Toby, she made her way to the bathroom. She sat on the toilet and closed her eyes. It was only when she opened them again that she noticed the blood in her underwear. She shouldn't be having her period. She was pregnant. She had read somewhere that some women spotted throughout their pregnancies, but this was not the case here. This was not spotting.

Olive swept her left foot closer to the bathroom door, the door opened farther. She could see Toby from where she was on the toilet. He was still asleep. Definitely good. She could not deal with him. Not right now. Another pain. Olive clutched her tummy. This couldn't be her period. If it was, this pain was something she wasn't accustomed to. Normally, she was grumpy during her time of the month, but rarely did she ever have to take something for discomfort. She counted to ten, then stood up. She wiped herself and then rummaged around in the bathroom until she found exactly what she needed: a sanitary napkin. She put one on. Tonya probably wouldn't notice, nor would Teal if it was hers.

She made her way back to the couch and slowly cuddled up against Toby. She was glad she wasn't alone. She hoped that Tonya and the baby were doing okay. Hard to believe that Teal was going to be a big sister. Things sure had changed a lot in the last couple of years. Olive and Teal were still friends and that was a good sign. Something she still appreciated—their friendship.

Suddenly it dawned on Olive. Maybe she was having a miscarriage! She quickly picked up her phone and Googled articles such as *signs you are having a miscarriage*. According to her calculation, she was between eight and ten weeks pregnant. Toby stirred in his sleep but his eyes remained shut. Good. She continued to scroll through articles. Within a half hour, she had her answer. There would be no hard choice to make. Olive would not have to decide if she wanted to keep the baby and raise it on her own, have the baby and give it up for adoption, or have an abortion. The choice—if you could even call it that—had been made for her. She had lost the baby. A tear from each cheek fell. It didn't matter that she hadn't known what she'd wanted. What mattered was the choice had been snatched away from her. She was no longer pregnant. How ironic that her best friend was at the hospital waiting to greet her new sibling, and here she was, having just lost her child. Olive quietly sobbed.

***

Olive must have drifted off to sleep. Next thing she knew, she felt something furry brush against her leg. She slowly opened one eye, then the other. Toby had a paintbrush in one hand and a jar of something else in the other. Just as he dipped the brush into the jar, Olive bolted straight up. What was he up to? Cripes. Had she actually fallen asleep while she babysat Toby? Not good at all. She listened for a moment, but didn't hear anything. The good news was, it was still just the two of them in the apartment. She fought back tears as she realized she needed to change her pad again.

"Hey, Toby. What'cha got there?" she asked. The last thing she wanted to do was to upset him.

"Paint!" He clapped his hands. This caused whatever was in the jar to slosh around and spill over the side of the jar.

Olive braced herself for blood red paint to appear.

Clear. The liquid coming out of the jar was clear. Lucky for her, Toby hadn't actually gotten into the paint yet.

"You want to paint, buddy?" Olive slowly rose from the couch. She felt somewhat better than she had earlier.

"Yep. Paint, please. I got the stuff. I just need colors now!" Toby walked toward the dining room table.

"Give me a minute and I will set everything up. I just have to go to the bathroom first."

"Okay, potty first." Toby nodded his head in her direction.

In the bathroom she changed the pad again. Maybe the whole thing was over. Not that it was something she would be able to forget anytime soon, but seeing the blood linger would just be a constant reminder. That was the last thing she needed.

- 14 -

TEAL COULDN'T BELIEVE HER BABY sister, Violet, had finally arrived. When her father had asked if she wanted to hold the baby, of course, she'd said "Yes!" But she couldn't believe how small the baby was compared to Toby. She was used to his weight in her arms, not a newborn baby's. After only a moment, it was clear that her father wanted the baby back. Although she was reluctant to hand the baby over, she did. It was time, anyway, for her to first call her mother to let her know the baby had arrived safely, and then to check in with Olive to see how she was faring with Toby.

***

"How are things going with Toby?"

"Things are good. We just started painting."

Normally Olive would have kept chatting. What

was going on with her. Teal thought it a bit strange. "Is everything okay, Olive? Is Toby giving you a hard time?" Teal couldn't think what else could be going on. Or maybe it had something had to do with Brad. Oh gosh. Not Brad. Teal couldn't deal with that crap now. All she wanted to do was bask in the sunlight of her new baby sister. Couldn't she just enjoy these moments?

"Nope," Olive responded.

A one-word answer. Olive had confirmed it. Teal knew for sure now that something was up. Part of her wanted to leave it alone but part of her knew it would keep bothering her until she found out was going on. Also, what if something major needed to be dealt with right now and couldn't wait? Teal decided not to take the chance.

"Olive. We've been friends for a long time. I don't believe you."

Nothing but silence on the other end for a full five seconds. In fact, Teal thought maybe they had been disconnected. She checked her phone but it looked like the two of them were still on the line.

"Olive? You there?"

"Yeah. Don't worry about things over here. Toby's fine. Is it there yet?"

"What?" Just like Olive to change topics. Good tactic.

"The baby!"

"Yes. And she's so cute. They named her Violet Teal Flint. Isn't that so cool? My name is her middle name."

"Baby! Baby! Baby!"

Teal laughed as she heard Toby squeal in the background. He must have heard Olive as they talked about the baby.

Teal heard Olive talking to Toby: "Yes, your baby sister is coming home soon."

She heard Toby clap his hands twice.

"Yippee! Tee?" Toby asked.

"Looks like he wants to chat with you, Teal. Is that okay?"

"Definitely. Put him on the phone." Of course Teal didn't mind spending a moment or two on the phone with Toby. That way, she'd even have more to report to her father. That worked out. Two birds with one stone kind of deal.

"Baby sister?" Toby asked.

"Yep. She's here and will be coming home soon. Now you make sure you're a good boy for Olive. Okay? Your baby sister will need a good brother. Can you do that, Toby?"

"Yes!" Toby exclaimed and clapped his hands again.

"Let me talk to Olive again. Ex Oh."

"Ess Oh."

Then Olive's voice. "It's me."

"Sounds like things are going good with Toby. But Olive, I wish you'd tell me what's going on with you. If it's Brad, just tell me."

"Why do you automatically think it has to do with Brad? I told you it's over between us. You honestly think I would go back to him after what he did to me? I cannot believe you would think that." Teal could hear Olive's deeply inhaled breath.

Teal tried smoothing things over. "Come on, Olive. I'm sorry but it's not like you haven't gone back to him before. I just want to make sure you're safe and okay. To me, if you're back with him, then you're not safe and you're far from okay. Okay?" She sensed that Olive wasn't really angry. It sounded like her friend was ready to break into sobs. They both had a lot on their plates right now.

"Just enjoy your time at the hospital with Violet and tell your dad and Tonya I said congrats. I will hold the fort down as long as they need me to."

"Thanks a bunch. I'll be home shortly to help out."

Teal hung up.

She had hoped to keep Olive on the phone longer, thinking her friend would eventually give in and tell her what was wrong, but the plan hadn't worked. Olive hadn't given her the slightest clue what might be going on. At least things seemed to be okay with Toby, and he wasn't giving Olive too much of a hard time. This was good. One less thing to worry about.

A few hours later, Teal's father indicated he wanted to spend the night at the hospital with the baby and Tonya. The hospital staff strongly discouraged him, and Tonya finally convinced him to go home since Toby was there, and it would be best if at least one of them was around for him. Obviously, for the moment, it couldn't be Tonya. It wasn't fair to expect both Olive and Teal to drop everything to look after Toby for them indefinitely even though Olive had said everything was going okay and that she didn't really mind staying. The fact was, Teal had already told her mother that she wouldn't be home tonight. She planned to spend the night at her father's to keep him company and to help with Toby.

- 15 -

TEAL HADN'T EVEN HAD TIME to take off her shoes before Toby barreled out of the kitchen. At least he had remembered to drop his paint brush on his picture before running up to her.

"Baby sister, baby sister." Toby looked around as he tugged on Teal's pants.

Teal's father scooped Toby into his arms, but Toby stared down the hallway toward the entrance door, seemingly determined to figure out where his baby sister was.

"You kids eat?" Teal's father inquired.

Olive shook her head. "I wasn't sure what time you'd be home."

Teal watched Olive. She hadn't been able to shake the feeling that something had happened while they'd been at the hospital.

Toby chipped in once again. "Baby sister, baby sister. Where baby sister?"

"He definitely seems ready to meet his baby sister," Teal said, laughing.

"Let's order in supper. Pizza good for everyone?" Teal's father waved his iPad.

Teal decided to let her father explain to Toby where his baby sister was. It would be easier that way.

"Your baby sister—her name is Violet—is with Mommy. They are sleeping at the hospital tonight, but will be home soon."

"Why is Mommy at hospital? Does she have a bobo?" Toby's eyes widened.

"A small one. She has a bobo because she had your baby sister. You remember her name is Violet?" Dad explained. Poorly.

"She is bad baby sister?" Toby's chin quivered. He was near tears. "Gave Mommy bobo?"

"No, Toby. She's not a bad baby sister." Teal said as she cleared the paint mess off the kitchen table to prepare a space for everyone to eat when the pizza arrived.

"You will stay for supper, won't you, Olive? I know it's late, but..." Dad turned to face Olive.

"I can't. But thanks for the offer. Lots of schoolwork to do. There's just never enough hours in the day." Olive picked up her shoes, put them on and started lacing them up.

Teal knew that Olive was lying through her teeth. Her father hadn't spent as much time with Olive as Teal's mother had. She knew her mother would have caught the lie in a heartbeat. Never had Olive ever used too much schoolwork as an excuse for anything in her entire life. School wasn't a priority for Olive. She did what she needed to get by and that was about it.

Just as Olive was about to leave, Teal hugged her and Teal was surprised that Olive held onto her longer than usual.

"Message me later and thanks a bunch for helping out with Toby," Teal told her.

"No worries. Can't wait to meet the new addition to the family. And yes, I'll message you later."

***

Throughout supper, Teal had waited for a message to come through from Olive. It hadn't. And now it was almost midnight and still nothing from Olive. Teal couldn't wait anymore. She had to send her a message because, if not, Olive would probably assume that Teal wasn't worried, and that simply wasn't true. Teal had been busy at the hospital with her sister, true, but she'd still known something was going on. Something that wasn't good. Something had upset Olive and it looked like whatever had happened, had nothing to do with Brad. Teal was definitely stumped.

I'll give you space if that's what you want. But I know
    something's wrong.-T

A half hour later Olive finally messaged her.

Thanks. Sorry.-O

It was unusual for Olive to apologize. Something that wasn't generally in her nature.

Olive, I am worried about you.-T
I lost it.-O

Well, Olive had every reason to have lost it, Teal thought. She had so much on her plate already. Add the fact that Brad, being an ass, had called from jail to talk to Olive's mom and had ratted Olive out. Not good. Not good at all. Teal empathized with her friend. Normally, Teal would trade places with her friend Olive in a heartbeat. Not this time. Currently her own life looked good compared to Olive's.

Don't be upset. It can't be helped.-T
How could you be so insensitive?-O
I don't mean to be. I'm just saying you have every right to be
    upset. You have a lot going on. What Brad did by
    calling your mom and telling her, was unforgivable.

And horrible. I can't even imagine what you are
going through.-T

A half hour went by and Olive had not replied. Teal
typed out another message.

What's going on, Olive? I just wanted to make sure you
were okay. Please tell me what I can do to help.-T
I'm sorry. I misunderstood what you said. I thought you were
happy about what happened with the baby.-O
The baby? Wha—?Oh my gosh. What happened? Are you
okay? What's going on? Want me to come over?-T
No! I don't want to be around anyone right now. I just need
to be left alone. The baby is gone.-O
Olive. Listen to me. The last thing I want to do is upset you
but I don't understand what you're talking about.
What happened?-T
I miscarried while you were at the hospital with Tonya.
Please. Please. I don't want to talk about it. No
matter what. Please don't make me.-O

Teal dropped her phone onto the bed. Oh my gosh.
As if. While she had been off helping—or at least being
there for Tonya at the hospital—Olive had been here.
Alone with Toby. And she had miscarried. How horrible it must have been. It had probably been for the
best but that wasn't the point. The point was the pain
Olive had endured on her own. In addition, how the
choice of what to do had been stolen from her.

Olive, I am so sorry. No matter what, I am so sorry. Let me
   know if there's anything I can do.-T

Teal waited an hour then gave up. No reply. Had Olive told her mother yet? Teal figured it was best for now if she left Olive alone. She would check in on her in the morning. That was all she could do.

- 16 -

AFTER TEAL HAD DEBATED MOST of the night, all the while tossing and turning, she decided it was best to show up at Olive's house unannounced. She was afraid that if Olive were forewarned, she wouldn't answer the door or, more likely, she'd make sure she wasn't at home in the first place. The element of surprise was best in any situation involving Olive.

Olive's mother opened the door after the first knock. Teal looked her up and down. She couldn't tell if she knew what had happened or not. Best to act like everything was cool. Cool. Yeah. She could play cool. No worries.

As Teal entered Olive's bedroom, Teal's cell phone went off. She quickly checked. It was a message from Jackson.

I was thinking, maybe I could go with you?-J
Where? To the prom?-T
Uh. No. To Spain! Spend time with you before classes
      start.-J

Teal didn't know what to reply. She wanted to take this trip on her own. Not with Jackson. Yikes. This was not something she had expected. Not at all. Why hadn't he brought up that idea months ago? Not now, with her leaving in a few weeks. Talk about waiting until the last minute. She inhaled deeply. For now, it didn't matter. She was here at Olive's. For Olive. The rest she would have to figure out later.

Olive was sitting on her bed wrapped in an old comforter Teal recognized from their younger days. Olive would always bring that very same pink-and-white-striped comforter with her on sleepovers.

Teal pointed at it. "Blast from the past, eh?"

"Hmm."

This was not a very good start. Teal sat on the edge of the bed.

Two full minutes went by during which neither of them said anything.

Finally, since she couldn't figure out what else to do, Teal moved in closer and pulled Olive into a hug. It wasn't long before Olive's shoulders started shaking and the tears came.

"It's going to be okay," Teal said. "I know it sucks right now, but it's going to be okay. It'll just take time. Maybe a lot of time. Well, maybe lots of time, but you know what I mean." Teal shush shushed her.

Olive sobbed so hard, she was gasping.

"I don't know how you feel and I'm not going to pretend I do. But I do know that the last few months have been crappy for you. Really crappy. This happened, and the stuff with Brad just added to it."

Teal pushed Olive back so she could glance around for a box of tissues. She spotted them on the dresser and released Olive to reachout for them. Olive grabbed a handful and blew her nose several times. *Better on the tissues than on me,* Teal thought.

Teal continued. "We have the prom next week. Hooray! Right?" She didn't feel all that enthusiastic herself about it right now, but needed to do something to get Olive to react. She didn't want to see Olive skip the prom and regret it later on, on top of everything else.

"Big whoop." Olive's eyes locked with hers.

"Come on. You have your dress and everything," Teal reminded her.

"Yeah, but I'm kinda short a date, remember? Brad's not supposed to be around me."

"Well, yes. There is that restraining order but that's beside the point. You need to let him go." Teal stood up and folded her arms across her chest.

"Easy for you to say. You have Jackson."

"Yep, and this is the first guy I have ever really dated. I waited a long time. Olive, you've dated a few and Brad is not the one for you. I may not have as much experience as you when it comes to relationships, but I know if a guy actually cares for you, he doesn't ever hit you. No matter *what*."

"I guess."

"You guess? You guess? What are you talking about? You think I'm making this up? That I'm lying?" Teal was getting more and more frustrated with her friend. Would she ever understand how bad Brad was for her?

"I just meant that you have Jackson. Who's amazing, by the way. And you're going on that trip. And you have a new sister. Lots of good things are going on for you. And my life is shit right now."

"I agree with you, Olive. Your life *is* shit right now. But why is it that way? Did you ever ask yourself that? Why?" By now, Teal was swaying back and forth from foot to foot. Things were getting heated.

Suddenly, Olive threw back the comforter and slid off the bed. She rose to her full height, angry eyes locked with Teal's. "Are you saying this is *my* fault? What kind of friend are you?"

Maybe it was time for Teal to speak up. Maybe it

was time to tell her friend, Olive, she needed to take responsibility for her own actions.

"The stuff with Brad, yes. He has treated you like crap from the beginning and you just kept going back. *That* is on you. He cheated on you and you took him back. *That* is on you, too. How did he treat you when he found out you were pregnant? What kind of guy does that?"

"I don't want to talk about it." Olive sat back down on the bed.

"Fine. We won't. I'm sorry about the baby, though. I truly am. But you deserve so much better than Brad, Olive. You're my friend. I want you to be happy and safe. You can't have those things with Brad or anyone else who treats you the way he did. You just can't."

"It's not fair!" Olive picked up her purse and threw it against the wall. *Thud.*

Within seconds, Olive's mother was in the room. "What's going on here? What are you two fighting about?"

"Nothing." Olive replied.

Teal stared at Olive. It wasn't Teal's place to say anything. This wasn't her mother and she wasn't Olive.

Olive's mother looked from Teal to Olive and back. Olive didn't say a word.

"I see. That's how it's going to be then. No one wants

to talk. Hmm Well, then. I think I shall sit here until someone does. Something is very wrong right here in Derry." She lowered herself to the computer chair and crossed her legs.

Teal couldn't help but smile. She hadn't heard Olive's mom use that quote in a long time. It was from one of Stephen King's movies. She and Olive had watched the movie *It* together several years ago. One weekend during the summer, the two of them had watched a dozen Stephen King movies and had picked up a few quotes they liked. She couldn't remember many of them now, but she remembered that one.

Olive was looking down so it was hard to read the expression on her face. Teal figured, if Olive's mom knew about the miscarriage, she would have already said something by now. So maybe she didn't know. However, it wasn't Teal's place to tell her, was it? It had to come from her own daughter.

No one said anything so being there was becoming awkward. Teal decided it was best if she broke the ice. She had nothing to lose.

"Olive, does your mom know?"

Olive's mother quickly glanced in Teal's direction.

Olive shook her head.

"Do I know what? Would someone tell me what is going on please?"

Olive's mother uncrossed her legs and now sat straight in the chair. Perhaps she sensed this was a more serious matter. Not just two friends arguing over a hot guy.

Olive's mom stared at her but Teal wasn't going to give it up. Olive was the one who had to tell her.

Olive shook her head again. Then, lifting her head and looking at her mother with tear-filled eyes, she spoke up. "The baby. Gone. Happy now?"

"What are you talking about?"

"I lost the baby. Gone. Poof. Hope you're happy now."

Olive's mother got up from the chair and went to the bed where Olive was slouched, before her eyes asked Teal a question.

Teal nodded yes, as in yes, it was true.

It was time for Teal to make her exit.

- 17 -

THE ISSUE WITH OLIVE HAD been taken care of, so now Teal had to figure out what to say to Jackson.

Very sweet of you! I will be okay on my own.-T
Oh. You don't want me to come with you?-J
It's not that. It's my first trip and I planned to go alone.-T

The last thing Teal wanted to do was have him be mad at her, especially with the prom exactly one week away. But at the same time, she planned on going to Spain alone. Her mother had gone with her to buy her plane tickets last month. Teal had made plans with Dottie. Everything was all set. She was good to go. By herself.

Okay. Fine then.-J

Teal was still new at relationships, but she knew that when she herself said something of that nature, it meant everything was far from "fine." Okay. So Jackson was upset. She couldn't do anything about it.

Will chat with you tonight. xo-T

Teal hoped he would be in a better mood when they chatted later. They usually spoke on the phone for several minutes before they went to bed.

Good. The limo company had confirmed the pick-up time for Jackson and her for prom night. Teal had already picked up her dress, a beautiful wine-red color. The dress hung waiting for her in its own sleek slip-cover. Teal had never owned anything so elegant. Jackson had rented a red Calvin Klein tuxedo to match. He wouldn't be able to pick up his tuxedo until the day before prom. Which was fine.

Shortly after supper Olive sent Teal a text message.

Thanks for today.-O
How are things? How are you doing?-T
Mom and I talked. Still hurts but better. If that makes any
        sense? lol-O
Yep! It does. I'm glad. Let me know if you need anything.-T
I won't be at school for the activities and stuff.-O
Are you going to be okay at home alone?-T
No worries. Mom is going to spend the day with me..-O

Awesome. Much needed, I think. Any plans?-T
Going to get my hair and nails done.-O
Take care of yourself.-T
I will. xo-O
xo-T

It would be a good starting-over point for Olive. Teal crossed her fingers that the togetherness of mom and daughter for the day would do them good. She couldn't remember the last time Olive had mentioned that she'd spent time with her mother.

After supper, she'd expected a text from Jackson as was usual, just to see what she was doing, but she didn't get one. Only because he was probably busy, she told herself and tried not to think about it. Instead, she focused on the prom and her upcoming trip. After prom, she would officially start counting down the days until she left. All she could think of was one word to describe how she felt: free. She couldn't wait to experience what that would actually feel like. Free from school, free from her parents, free from Jackson, free from everything.

After watching an episode of *The Walking Dead*, Teal decided to hop in the shower and then, if she hadn't received a text from Jackson, she would just call. Easier that way.

So of course, she showered more quickly than usual

and stubbed her toe as she tried to hurry out of the bathroom to get to her room and check her phone, but no message. No matter, she told herself as she hurriedly dried herself and grabbed a pair of pajamas out of the drawer and slipped them on.

No answer. She ended up calling Jackson three times and all three times the call had gone straight to voicemail. She tried to convince herself he was busy; but deep down, she wondered if maybe he didn't want to talk to her. Maybe he really was mad because she wanted to go on this trip alone. That was silly. Wasn't it? But what if he was? And what if they ended up breaking up? Or not going to the prom together? What would she do then? She let out a small sob. As if this would really happen. Maybe things were too good to be true.

Next morning, the first thing Teal did was check her phone to see if there was a message from Jackson. Nothing. She didn't want to move or get out of bed, but she had to. Today, she was going to her father's to spend the night. Probably one of the second or last times she would see everyone at her father's place before she left for her trip. Months ago, her trip seemed like it was years away. Hard to believe, that this time next month, she would be in another country, exploring on her own. She couldn't wait. School was pretty much over. The prom was in a couple of days. Everything was nearly perfect. Except with whatever was going on between Jackson and her. Whatever that was. She was going to be away for an entire month. Maybe she would leave and he would break up with her through text. All these what ifs were driving her nuts. She got out of bed to get ready to go visit her father.

- 18 -

TOBY SEEMED TO BE EXTRA happy to see her. No doubt because her father and Tonya were busy with Violet and didn't have as much time for one-on-one with him. After she had read him a third book, Teal suggested he get out his coloring stuff to make a picture for his baby sister.

Toby jumped at the idea.

That was good. Seeing Toby was great, but she also wanted to spend time with Violet as well.

Violet's little fingers were curled around Teal's left index finger even though the baby was sound asleep. Toby was working hard on a second picture for his sister. And Teal's father and Tonya had gone for a quick coffee to get out for a bit of a respite, just the two of them. So far so good.

***

It had been an hour and nothing major had happened. Teal had everything under control and sighed contentedly. She would miss these two while she was gone. Not too much would change with Toby, but the baby would grow while she was in Spain.

Then. A text message! From Jackson!

She stared at the phone wanting to read the message but worried about what it would say. Did she dare? She did.

Hey, is the limo and stuff confirmed for the prom?-J

This was a good sign. Wasn't it? Unless he'd decided he wasn't going to the prom and wanted her to cancel everything. Only one way to find out. She muttered to herself that it wasn't easy to type a text with your fingers crossed.

Yes. We're all set to go for the big day!-T
Good. Just thought I'd check.-J
xo-T

Teal let out the sigh she had been holding in that she hadn't been aware of. So far so good, the two of them were still going to the prom.

***

Teal's father took Violet from Teal.

"You excited about your trip?" he sked. "It's coming

up right after the prom, isn't it?"

"I can hardly sleep sometimes. Can't believe every-thing that's going on: prom, the trip, college."

"We'd love to see you before you leave for your trip. How about I pick you up the night before you head out? Then, if you like, you can spend the night here and we can take you to the airport? That way, everybody'll get to see you before you leave. How's that sound?"

Teal had figured this would have been the last time she'd see them all before she left, but if he wanted to see her one more time again, that was fine by her.

"Sure, Dad, that would be great."

The phone buzzed. Teal looked down to see who it was. A message from Jackson. Teal quickly checked it.

Can we meet up?-J
Sure. When?-T
Now? I could come over to your place?-J
I can't. –T
But you just said sure. Why can't you? Where are you?-J
I thought you meant later today. Or maybe tomorrow.-T
I thought maybe we could talk.-J
Okay. Go ahead.-T
I don't want to do it through text, Teal. In person.-J

This did not sound good. Teal didn't want to meet up with Jackson now. Whatever he wanted to talk about couldn't be good. Not if he wanted to do it in person. Not to mention he'd seemed very persistent.

I'm spending the night at my dad's.-T
Okay. I'll come over there.-J

Since she wasn't sure what he had to say, Teal thought maybe it wasn't the best idea for Jackson to come to her father's place. Her father liked him and all, but she wasn't sure what was going on.

How about I meet you at the Second Cup close to Dad's?-T
I can be there in a half hour.-J
I was thinking more tonight. Like around 8 pm?-T
I guess.-J
Sounds good. See you later. xo-T
kk-J

Now Teal was definitely worried. This wasn't the Jackson she knew. What was so important that he had to talk to her tonight? If he was excited about something, he sure as heck didn't seem like it. She checked the time and it was only 3 pm. She still had a couple of hours to go until supper, and then get through the meal, and then play with the kids for a bit and then it would be their bedtime and then after all that, it would be time to go meet Jackson. And then. And then. And then. It was going to be a long day.

She tried to keep busy. She read more books to

Toby than she could keep track of. That helped some. She spent a lot of time with the baby.

Then finally, it was time to meet with Jackson.

- 19 -

TEAL ARRIVED BEFORE JACKSON DID so the waiting made her tension worse, but when he got there, she hugged him, noting that nothing seemed unusual. Good sign.

She waited. He was the one who wanted to meet up. He should start the conversation.

"Thanks for agreeing to meet me here." He smiled, but somehow it wasn't the same.

"Welcome." Whatever he had to say to her, she had no desire to make it easier on him.

"Here it is, Teal. I am just going to come right out and say it." Jackson paused.

Teal inhaled a deep breath and let it out slowly. She had to stay composed.

"I just don't get why I can't come with you on the

trip. How come you don't want me to come with you?" He actually looked sad.

Teal shrugged her shoulders. She took a moment before speaking. The last thing she wanted to do was make things worse by saying stuff she didn't mean just because she was upset.

"It has nothing to do with you, Jackson. I just want to go alone. This is what Miss Tate wanted. For me to experience freedom. For me to go and see *my* house by *myself.* To go and explore just a sliver of this world before I head off to college."

"You still need to make a choice about college."

"I have made my choice. I put in my acceptance today."

"That's great," Jackson said, smiling. "I'm happy for you! What have you decided?"

"I'll be the taking the Social Work Program, the three-year one at Algonquin. My specialty for my third year will be working with seniors." Her parents knew she'd made that decision and so did Olive, but Teal herself was still in shock. It felt nice to brag. She'd worked hard and it had paid off.

Now for the hard part. Teal needed to just put it out there. Say it now. Get it over with.

"If it's over between us just because you can't come with me on my trip, then I'm sorry it has to be that way.

I thought I knew you better than that." She looked down at the floor, not trusting herself not to cry.

"What are you talking about? I wasn't going to break up with you just because you won't let me tag along with you on your trip. That's ridiculous!"

She didn't know what to say. She hadn't seen him like this before.

"Am I upset? Yeah. Why? Because I'm going to miss you. And I have to admit that I'm jealous." He grinned. "But that's it. I'm not going anywhere. I'll be right here waiting when you get back." He grasped her hand and squeezed it.

What a relief, she thought. She was lucky to have him.

"One more thing we need to talk about, though. The prom."

Oh, she'd almost forgotten about that. Well, not the prom itself, but the after part. How was she going to deal with that? She cared for Jackson—there was no doubt about that—but she didn't believe she was ready to share her entire self with him yet. "Okay. What about it?"

"Our parents know we're going to the prom. They know we didn't do anything special for mine last year. I'm not sure what your mother thinks but my mom's afraid I might do something stupid at a party after the prom. You know."

Teal knew.

"Therefore, she has come up with a compromise. She knows I can go to a hotel or whatever." He paused as though he were looking for the right word, wanting to make sure the next part came out right.

Ha! Teal thought. He'd been thinking about getting a hotel! Cripes. Now what was she going to do? She didn't trust herself to go to a hotel. There would be even more pressure.

"Teal? You listening?"

"Yeah. Yes, I am."

"So Mom suggested that instead of us being who-knows-where at all hours of the night, that you spend the night at my place instead. And don't worry, Mom won't be there."

Teal raised her eyebrows in a question. So the plan was for her to go and spend the night at Jackson's after Prom and his mother would disappear for the night? Where would his mother go? And did she have any chance at all of her own mother agreeing to this plan?

"Where's your mom going to go? I'm not sure my mother will agree to this."

"Our mothers have already talked about it. Not going to lie to you. At first, your mom said no flat out. Then I guess my mom explained to her all the stuff we could be doing elsewhere, unsupervised, with a bunch of other people who may or may not be as well-behaved as we are. Then she agreed."

"She did?" A laugh burst out of Teal. "You have to be kidding me!"

"Yep. It will be just you and me. I swear, no pressure. It'll be nice with neither of us having to leave for curfew."

Teal was still nervous but at least she wouldn't have to battle a hotel scene. She knew her way home from Jackson's. Just in case.

- 20 -

THE PERFECT SONG TO END the dance was "I'll Never Love Again" by Lady Gaga. The limo ride had been awesome. Olive had found a date at the last minute and she and her date seemed to have hit it off. This was good. Teal knew Olive was trying to keep her mind busy.

They had taken photo upon photo using props, all kinds of silly things to mark this special occasion. An occasion that should be marked and remembered. Teal had no idea what Olive was doing after the actual prom itself, but figured it was none of her business. As far as Teal herself was concerned, she was nervous about things to come later on in the evening between Jackson and her, of course, but she was looking forward to it. Teal could hardly believe she was actually done with high school. She had graduated. She was moving on to the next phase of her life: college. She had so much to look forward to. It was hard to believe that only a year ago, she was having a hard time seeing the tunnel, let alone the light at the end of it.

***

As soon as they entered Jackson's house, the butterflies let loose in Teal's stomach. Jackson had said many times that there would be no pressure; just the two of them, and it would be nice and quiet.

The pull-out couch was already set up with lots of pillows, and on the coffee table was a bunch of small candles all lined up. Everything was cozy and inviting.

"So far so good?" Jackson asked.

Teal tossed him a relieved smile. "So far so good."

"There's a fruit and cheese plate in the fridge and some other munchies on the kitchen counter."

Teal opened the fridge. Inside was the platter and plenty of options for drinks as well: sparkling water, four kinds of pop, two different juices and a caesar 4-pack. On the kitchen counter were four bags of chips.

"Do you think we have enough stuff to eat tonight?" Teal laughed.

"Yeah," said Jackson. "She went a bit overboard. But for breakfast, all you get is coffee or tea and a muffin. Just a head's up about that." He pulled her into his arms. They kissed. Twice.

Earlier that week they had discussed what they might wear to bed. Going to bed fully clothed seemed somewhat silly. Especially since they didn't know when they would have another chance at a night to themselves like this. It hadn't taken them long to come to the conclusion that even the *idea* of going to bed completely naked would make them both uncomfortable.

In the end, Jackson suggested he wear pajama bottoms and she wear one of his T-shirts as a nightgown. He had promised no pressure, and true to form, Jackson kept his word.

In no time, they were cuddled together on the pullout couch, watching one of Teal's all-time-favorite movies, *The Goonies.*

Knowing it was one of her faves, Jackson had bought a copy just so they could watch it together on their special night. Thinking of how Jackson was always thoughtful where she was concerned, made her smile.

Her happy sigh prompted Jackson to ask, "Is everything all right?"

"I'm just so happy right now, Jackson. Everything feels right. It's hard to explain."

"I'm glad." He kissed her lips then brushed her cheek.

Teal pointed at the TV. "This is the character I was

talking about. They call him Chunk."

Jackson turned his attention back to *The Goonies*.

***

An hour into the movie, Teal was startled by a snore. She turned to find Jackson asleep beside her, his arm thrown over her stomach. She wriggled slightly, hoping to wake him up, but it didn't work.

When the movie was over, she turned off the TV and blew out the last candle. And that was the end of their evening.

Teal wasn't certain if she were irritated or relieved that Jackson had fallen asleep during their special evening. Was she irritated because she'd anticipated the two of them staying up chatting, fooling around and watching movies till the sun came up? That's how special nights ended in the movies, wasn't it? Was she relieved because she hadn't had to make the big decision about going all the way with Jackson? Had the choice been made for her? No. She could have tried harder to wake him, couldn't she? That had to be a sign that she was, in fact, *not* ready. Wasn't it?

- 21 -

THE DAY HAD FINALLY ARRIVED. After all the plans and counting down she had done, it was here. Teal was about to start another chapter in her life. Alone. And she couldn't wait.

Teal's father threw his arm over her shoulder and said, "How about a picture like this, Jackson? With Teal in the middle." To Teal, he said, "You have to be in the middle or else the picture won't look right."

Teal rolled her eyes. She had to pose for yet another picture? She inhaled deeply, but her mother raised her eyebrows at her, so she let the breath out slowly and with a sheepish grin. A few more photos, some more goodbyes, and that would be it. A few minutes of annoyance for a month of freedom. *I can handle this.*

It seemed weird to see her parents together. They'd

both attended her high school graduation, but still, it was something that would take getting used to. She supposed it would've been easier without Tonya being there with Toby and Violet, but they were all present.

More than anything, she appreciated that Jackson had switched shifts at the computer store he was working at so he could say goodbye to her at the airport. She'd told him not to bother. Her whole family—*both* families—would be there so it would just be annoying anyway. He'd said okay, but then he showed up at the last minute. Teal had been surprised but glad at the same time.

Teal hugged her mother goodbye first. They hadn't been spending a lot of time together lately and she felt somewhat guilty about that, but she wasn't a high-school kid anymore, was she? She promised herself she'd send a postcard shortly after her arrival in Spain. She'd say something sweet or maybe she'd send flowers, just because.

Next, her father. They'd become closer than when her parents were together. This was probably due to all the changes in his life and his wanting to include Teal in it that brought them together more. She'd miss him. And his yummy pancakes.

Tonya hugged her and smiled. It was hard to believe that at one point, Teal hadn't wanted Tonya to be a part of her life. If it weren't for Tonya, Teal wouldn't have Toby, or Violet. Right now, she couldn't imagine her life without Toby or the baby.

Teal bent down to give her little brother a high-five. "Remember what Daddy's supposed to practice making while I'm gone?"

"Pancake!" Toby clapped his hands and lunged forward to hug Teal.

Teal closed her eyes. The tears were there. Right there fighting to be released, but she wouldn't let them. Not now. Not in front of everybody. She picked Toby up and squeezed him gently. She'd miss the others, sure she would, but she was certain she'd miss Toby the most. And Jackson! But there was no way she would ever say anything like that out loud.

Next, she held Violet for a moment, staring down at the sweet innocent bundle in her arms. She kissed her forehead before she passed her back to Tonya. No doubt Violet would look different, maybe even be making her first cooing baby talk sounds by the time Teal returned from her trip.

Jackson grabbed her hands in his and everyone else stepped back to give them space. He kissed each of her hands then their eyes locked. Teal was having even greater difficulty holding her tears back.

"This is it," he said. "What you've been waiting for.

Go for it. But be careful, okay?" He grinned then kissed her quickly on the lips.

Teal bowed her head. This was it. She held her head high as she smiled at everyone. They had closed the gap again and were all crowded around her once more.

"Goodbye. I'll miss you lots, but I'll be in touch soon as I can. I'll be home to bug you all before you know it!"

Teal was scared and nervous and she knew everybody knew she was, but she still didn't want to show it.

Then a familar female voice: "Go for it!" It was Olive, yelling as she ran toward Teal. "You can do anything. *The scariest moment is always just before you start. After that, things can only get better.* Stephen King wrote that!" She swept Teal into a big hug.

"You made it!"

"I did, didn't I?" Olive said, all out of breath. "I had to see you before you left, silly. Don't forget me while you're gone, eh?"

As Teal walked backwards toward the line of travelers boarding her flight, Olive blew her a kiss.

"I won't," she called back, then turned toward the next chapter of her life.

This is it. She was ready.

Acknowledgements

To write it a book takes more than just an idea, time, and words. It takes patience, friends, and guidance from a small team of people.

I would like to thank Sherrill Wark, Phyllis Bohonis and Dakota Morgan. Thank you for your time, thoughts, and encouragement.

About the Author

Catina Noble's writing started appearing in late 2009. To date, Catina has more than 200 publications including her poetry, short stories, articles/interviews, and her photos.

When she is not writing or creating new art work, she teaches mixed media art to children, practices art journaling, volunteers time in the community, and plots her next set of adventures. In 2009, Catina graduated from Carleton University with a B.A.

Writing is her first love and then art.

Other Works by Catina Noble

Cat's Journals: *I'm Glad I Didn't Kill Myself*
and *Lost at 13*
Vacancy at the Food Court (collection of short stories)
Katzenjammer (collection of poetry)
Not Just Me, Not Again (trilogy parts 1 and 2)

Catina Noble's short stories and poetry have
appeared in:

*Chicken Soup for the Soul, Woman's World Magazine,
Bywords, The Steel Chisel,* Canadian Authors
Association–National Capital Region's *Byline*
magazine, *Short-Story-Me, Riverview Park Review,
Charlatan, Mainstreeter, Canadian Newcomer
Magazine, Y Travel Blog, Mojito Mother, Cocoa
Cabin, Scarlet Thistles, Lemon Trade Winds,* the
*Mindful Word, Pussyfoot, Curious the Tourist Guide,
Encompass IV, Image, Aborealis* and
Prairie Fire Journal